Disciplining
YOUNG CHILDREN

by Kristin Thoennes Keller

Consultant:
Ann Michelle Daniels, PhD
Family Life, Parenting, and Child Care
Specialist/Assistant Professor
South Dakota State University

SKILLS
FOR
TEENS
WHO
PARENT

LifeMatters
an imprint of Capstone Press
Mankato, Minnesota

LifeMatters Books are published by Capstone Press
PO Box 669 • 151 Good Counsel Drive • Mankato, Minnesota 56002
http://www.capstone-press.com

SPECIAL ADVISORY: The information within this book concerns sensitive and important issues about which parental and teen discretion is advised. Because this book is general in nature, the reader should consult an appropriate health, medical, or other professional for advice. The publisher and its consultants take no responsibility for the use of any of the materials or methods described in this book nor for the products thereof.

Printed in the United States of America

Library of Congress Cataloging-in-Publication Data
Thoennes Keller, Kristin.
      Disciplining young children / by Kristin Thoennes Keller.
          p.   cm.—(Skills for teens who parent)
      Includes bibliographical references and index.
      ISBN 0-7368-0701-2 (book)
      1. Discipline of children—Juvenile literature. 2. Teenage parents—Juvenile literature.
      [1. Discipline of children. 2. Teenage parents.] I. Title. II. Series.
      HQ770.4 .T49 2001
      649´.64—dc21
                                    00-032750
                                    CIP

      Summary: A guide for teenage parents. Defines discipline, explains child temperaments, and gives advice on how to avoid problem behaviors and what to do when they occur.

Staff Credits
Rebecca Aldridge, editor; Adam Lazar, designer; Kim Danger, photo researcher

Photo Credits
Cover: Uniphoto/©Michael A Keller, large; PNI/©David Young-Wolff, top; ©StockByte, middle; ©DigitalVision, bottom
©DigitalVision, 6
International Stock/©Bon, 20; ©James Davis, 59
©Kimberly Danger, 13, 54
Photo Agora/©Robert Maust, 56
Photo Network/©Eric R. Berndt, 17; ©Esbin-Anderson, 25; ©Ted Schmoll, 44; ©Myrleen Ferguson Cate, 46
Unicorn Stock Photos/©N. P. Alexander, 22; ©Phyllis Keal, 38
Uniphoto/©Dave Porter, 10; ©Daniel Grogan, 18; ©Llewellyn, 30, 33; ©Terry Way Photography, 37; ©Jackson Smith, 49
Visuals Unlimited/©N. P. Alexander, 8; ©Nancy Alexander, 41; ©Deneve Feigh Bunde, 51

Table of Contents

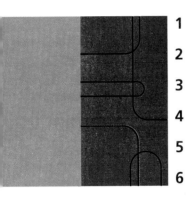

- Discipline is a relationship between parent and child that begins at birth.

- Discipline is about nurturing and guiding your child, not just correcting misbehavior. You can learn ways to nurture and guide your child.

- Connecting with your baby at birth helps him to trust you. This trust is important for later discipline.

- You can learn healthy ways to teach and nurture your infant.

- Responding quickly when your baby cries is one important way to build trust.

CHAPTER 1

Introduction to Discipline

Discipline is a relationship between parent and child that begins at birth. Infants who feel secure and attached to their parents are likely to behave well later on. The way parents interact with their newborn can affect his future behavior. In this chapter, you will learn a positive way of thinking about discipline. You will learn why and how to attach with your baby.

Discipline Is Teaching

The word *discipline* actually comes from a Latin word that means "to teach." You are your child's first teacher in life. The way you discipline your child helps her learn how to act. Sometimes parents think discipline is only about punishment. Discipline gives your child tools for the future; punishment does not.

Discipline is about your relationship with your child. Use discipline to nurture and guide your child, as well as to correct her behavior. To nurture means to meet the needs of your child to help her grow and develop. The next sections discuss nurturing and guiding. You will read more about correcting misbehavior in Chapter 4.

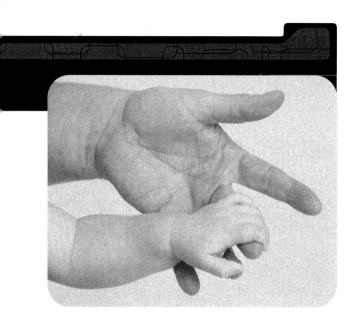

Nurturing Your Child

Children learn best when they know they are loved and supported. Here are some ways you can nurture your child:

- Love your child, no matter what his behavior.

- Listen to your child.

- Expect the best from your child, but be understanding when your child can't do his best.

- Try to understand your child's behavior.

- Be a good role model for your child.

- Make sure your child is safe both physically and emotionally.

- Tell your child you appreciate the good behaviors.

Most children who develop strong and secure attachments with their parents grow up to be confident and caring.

Guiding Your Child

Children need help managing their actions and feelings. They need help learning responsibility. Parents should have a few important rules about behavior, and children should know what the rules are. Children also need to know what will happen if rules are broken. Here are some ways to help guide your child:

- Prepare your child for difficult situations.

- Help your child learn to calm down.

- Give your child a chance to do something the right way.

- Take your child away from situations that she cannot handle.

- Show your child how to do things.

- Model appropriate behavior for your child.

- Help your child learn to solve problems.

- Say yes as often as you can. Say no only when you have to.

- Make your child's environment one she can explore safely without restriction.

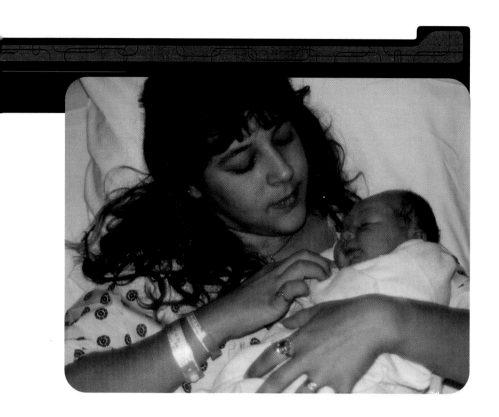

"I read a book about parenting before Mickey was born. It talked about attaching with your baby as soon as possible after birth. I'm glad I read it. I was able to breastfeed Mickey right away. I asked the nurse to wait before putting in the eye ointment that all babies need. The book said that the ointment makes the baby's vision blurry. I wanted Mickey to be able to look at me for a while first.

"The nurse was cool about it. She said she could wait to use the ointment for up to an hour. The book said to hold your baby 12 to 18 inches from your face. That's because babies are nearsighted when they're born. So, I held Mickey close and we watched each other the whole time."

Attachment and Trust Beginning at Birth

It's important to attach with your baby as early as possible. Try to hold him as soon as you can after birth. Gaze into his eyes and talk to him in a soothing voice. Try to keep him in the room with you throughout the hospital stay. Instead of having nurses change his diaper and bathe him, have them supervise while you do it. Avoid having too many distracting visitors.

Doing these things right away will help you and your baby attach. Attaching early is important for both you and your baby. It allows the relationship between parent and child to begin unfolding. Your baby will learn to trust you. That trust is important later when your child becomes more independent. Teaching him this early trust is part of discipline.

Sometimes babies need to stay at the hospital for a longer period of time because of medical resons. If this happens with your baby, don't worry about attachment. You still can form an attachment with him later.

Parents who have a connection with their infant can develop a disciplined relationship with their child. As time passes, connected parents are better able to express their expectations. Connected children are better able to understand those behaviors expected of them. This type of relationship is healthier than one in which there is little trust.

Teaching and Nurturing Babies Up to 9 Months

How you discipline your child depends on her age. In the beginning, you teach and nurture your child. This allows you to develop a healthy discipline relationship as your child gets older.

Knowing about child development is important. It can help you learn appropriate ways to teach, nurture, and discipline your child at certain ages. For more information on development, see the books *Parenting an Infant* and *Parenting a Toddler* in this series. The following is a list of some developmental characteristics in babies up to 9 months:

- They use their mouth to explore their world.

- They cry to tell you what they need.

- They learn to talk by listening and responding to the people who are around them.

- They need to feel safe, secure, and loved.

Knowing these facts about your baby can help you teach and nurture her in a healthy and effective way. The following list provides appropriate ways to teach and nurture babies up to about 9 months. Parenting in these ways builds on the foundation of trust that began at birth.

- Give your baby lots of attention and loving affection. You cannot spoil your child at this stage. The more attention you give her, the better.

- Never shake or hit your baby. Ask someone you trust to care for your baby for a while if you feel overwhelmed. Or, put her in her crib to give yourself a break.

- Put unsafe things out of your baby's reach. Babies want to explore their world. Help your baby to explore in a safe way without too many restrictions.

- Offer your baby something in place of an item you do not want her to have. Babies feel frustrated when you simply say no and take away something. To keep her from getting upset, offer your baby a safe object for her to explore. This technique is called redirection. It's an important strategy to use even as she gets older.

- Have routine in your day. This helps your baby know what to expect. Babies who know what to expect have an easier time adjusting to change during the day.

- Move your baby if she is getting into something she shouldn't. Again, do not simply move her away. Instead, redirect her to a different area of interest. Encourage her exploration of acceptable areas.

Crying is your baby's way of talking to you. She'll cry when she's hungry. She'll cry when she needs to be held. She may cry when too many people are talking to her. She will cry if something makes her uncomfortable, such as a wet diaper or an upset tummy.

Responding to Your Baby's Needs

Some people may tell you that you'll spoil your baby by holding him too much. They might say you will spoil him by picking him up too quickly when he cries. This isn't true. Babies in this age group communicate by crying. They have no other way to let you know what they need. You should pick up your newborn whenever he cries. If you don't, he will be discouraged. He'll learn that communicating doesn't meet his needs. He may be likely to try unhealthy behaviors for attention when he is older.

Meeting your baby's needs quickly in the early months helps to develop good communication between you and him. He will learn trust. Remember that this trust is important in the first stages of discipline. As your child gets older, you can move on to setting limits. This is discussed more in Chapter 3.

A Final Word

Discipline is meant to be a positive relationship between you and your child. Discipline is not about spanking, yelling, or putting someone in a corner. It isn't about saying no all the time. It isn't about always giving your child a time-out. Discipline is about the loving, trusting, and respectful relationship you can have with your child.

The goal of discipline is to help your child become responsible for her own behavior. Infants and toddlers need you to be patient, gentle, and understanding as they learn what is and is not acceptable. You can teach through example. You can guide your child in ways that make her feel accepted and able. You can help your child be the best she can be.

POINTS TO CONSIDER

Has your understanding of discipline changed after reading this chapter? Explain.

Why is it important to attach with your baby as soon as possible after birth?

What are some things parents should know about babies from birth to 9 months? What are some appropriate ways to teach and nurture babies in this age group?

What can you teach your child by quickly responding to his cries?

■ All babies are born with their own temperament. Some temperaments are more challenging for parents than others are.

■ Researchers have labeled nine temperament traits that children have. Knowing your child's temperament can help you to be a better parent and respond effectively to certain behaviors.

■ Accepting your child's temperament is as important as understanding it. Parents who try to change their child's temperament are not accepting of it. You can help your child be her best by accepting her temperament.

CHAPTER 2

Understanding Your Child's Temperament

People often think a "good baby" is one who doesn't cry much or one who sleeps through the night. In truth, no babies are good or bad. All babies simply are born with their own temperament. Temperaments are qualities and characteristics that contribute to one's personality. Some temperaments are more challenging for parents than others are. This chapter will help you to understand and accept your child's temperament. It also will offer suggestions for working with that temperament.

The Nine Temperament Traits

Parents can benefit from understanding their child's temperament. Parents who understand their child can respond positively to her in a way that encourages development and growth. Parents who accept their child's temperament can help her reach her full potential.

Dr. Stella Chess and Dr. Alexander Thomas studied the personalities of children for a long period of time. These researchers came up with nine temperament traits that children might have. The following sections describe those temperament traits.

A key to understanding your child is understanding her temperament.

Activity Level

Activity level refers to how much and how often your child moves around. Infants with high activity levels might not like to sit in an infant swing. Instead, they may like to be on the floor where they can move about freely. Infants with low activity levels may enjoy just watching the action around them. They often choose to sit still, even though they are able to move.

Parents should respect their child's activity level. Parents of active children should plan to sit at the back during an event so their child can move around. Parents with low activity level children should pay lots of attention to these children who don't seem to need much motion. These children still need stimulation even though you don't have to chase them around.

CALISTA, AGE 16

"My sister's baby hardly ever moves. He is 13 months and just sits still in the middle of the floor, smiling at everyone. My 10-month-old never stops moving. She is almost walking. She never sat in a swing for more than 5 minutes at a time. When I take her in a stroller, she cries to get out after just a few blocks. When I was pregnant, she didn't stop moving either. Maybe she'll be a dancer when she grows up!"

Rhythmicity

Rhythmicity refers to how predictable your child's biological functions are. Biological functions include things such as sleeping, eating, and going to the bathroom. Some children prefer to eat a big breakfast and then nibble the rest of the day. Other children, however, might not have any regular eating pattern. Some children have a bowel movement every morning. Others have no regularity in passing their body's solid waste.

Parents with high rhythmicity children should try to follow their children's patterns. If you know your child always needs a nap right after lunch, don't schedule any appointments during that time. Parents with less predictable children shouldn't have high expectations. Mealtimes and toilet training are just two examples of situations that will be unpredictable. Parents of low rhythmicity children should learn to expect the unexpected.

Approach or Withdrawal

This temperament trait refers to the way your child reacts immediately to new situations. These situations might include being introduced to new people, foods, places, or toys. Children who respond by approaching may reach for the new food or smile at the new person. Children who respond by withdrawing may turn away or cry when seeing a new face. They may spit out a new food when tasting it.

Parents with children who approach may have an easier time introducing new situations. Just make sure to keep such an adventurous child safe. Parents with children who are slow to warm up to new things should respect those children. Introduce new food with familiar food. For example, put a new strained vegetable on familiar bits of toast. Give the child a chance to adjust to a stranger or person she hasn't seen for a while. Show her that you trust the person. She will warm up according to her own timeline.

Adaptability

Adaptability refers to how your child reacts over time to new situations. Some children may continue to cry long after their parent has left them at day care. These children may continue to do this every day for weeks. Other children stop crying within a few minutes of their parent's departure. These children eventually don't cry when they arrive at day care. Some children spit out a new food the first few times but eventually eat it. Others accept a new food far more slowly, if at all.

Parents with children who adapt well to changes have little trouble with new situations. However, parents of children who are slow to adapt should introduce change slowly. For example, stay at a new day care with your child for at least 20 minutes each day before leaving. Put a tiny portion of a new food on her plate, but don't expect your child to eat it. Respect that your child needs time to adjust to change.

Some babies are open to just about any new experience. They don't mind new food, new people, or new places. Other babies have a hard time with new things. This is because all babies are born with a unique personality.

Sensory Threshold

This temperament trait refers to how strongly your child reacts to sensory input. This input has to do with things such as touch, sound, sight, smell, and taste. Some children need silence to sleep while others can sleep through anything. Some children can crawl across a hardwood floor with no problem. Others, however, may not like the feel of the hardwood on their knees.

Parents of children with a high sensory threshold notice that these children have little trouble with sensory input. If your child has a low sensory threshold, however, try to respect it. Keep the music down when she sleeps. Don't expect her to crawl across the grass if she seems to dislike the tickling feeling.

WESTON, AGE 19

"My son, Bart, seems to have a low sensory threshold. He seems especially sensitive to texture and taste. Bart seemed comfortable eating baby food, but he hated it when we introduced the thicker foods for older babies. Now he's old enough to eat finger foods. When we introduce something new, we don't expect him to even touch it until he's ready. We just put little bits on Bart's tray until he decides he can handle it. And he usually does, in time."

Quality of Mood

This temperament trait refers to your child's general mood. Some children have sunny attitudes and smile and laugh a lot. Other children, however, have a tendency to cry or yell immediately when disappointed, sad, or angry.

Parents of children with happy moods should enjoy it. Often these children can teach their parents something about seeing the positive in life. If you are the parent of a child who is less cheerful, you shouldn't take it personally. Your child simply is who she is. Try to be sensitive to her moods. Give her extra loving attention when she seems to need it. Share your good moods with her.

Intensity of Reaction

This temperament trait refers to how your child responds to events around her. Some children cry for several minutes if another child takes a toy away. Other children may yell once and then move on to something new. Some children seem to cry at every little bump or scrape. Others rarely cry even at what seems like a painful injury.

Parents of children with low intensity of reaction know that when their children cry, it probably is serious. Parents of children with high intensity of reaction should teach their children to cope with disappointment, pain, and change. These parents also need to be careful to not treat lightly something that is quite serious. Just because your child may cry at every injury doesn't mean the next one won't be serious.

Distractibility

Distractibility refers to how an outside stimulus, or source of excitement, can affect your child's behavior. It also refers to how easily your child can be distracted. Some babies can breastfeed comfortably during a basketball game. Other babies cannot breastfeed if someone besides the mother is in the same room.

Parents of an easily distracted child simply should distract their child when she is heading toward something unsafe. Parents of a child who is not easily distracted have to be more creative. Your child may insist on heading for the VCR every time she is in the living room. If so, consider moving the VCR up high until she's older, or be prepared to stop her every time. If your child cries whenever you take away something she shouldn't have, offer something else to help distract her.

Persistence and Attention Span

These two characteristics usually are related. Persistence refers to your child's desire to continue an activity even though something or someone tries to stop her. Attention span refers to the length of time she pursues an activity without interruption. Some children can play with one toy for half an hour. Other children move from toy to toy, spending only minutes with each one.

If asked, most parents and teachers would prefer children with long attention spans and high persistence. These children usually are easy to teach and entertain. However, few children fit that description.

Parents of children with persistence and a long attention span may be able to accomplish a lot of work while their children play. Parents of the opposite kind of children, however, have to keep hopping. Your child may have low persistence and a short attention span. If so, have new objects and activities on hand for your child to explore and discover. Closely monitor her to make sure she is safe.

Goodness of Fit

This concept is related to the temperament traits. Goodness of fit refers to how a child's temperament matches her environment. It's important for you to make adjustments in your child's surroundings to better suit her temperament traits.

Goodness of fit also refers to how a child's temperament harmonizes with her parent's temperament. Your child is not the only one with a temperament. You have one, too! Because of differences in your temperaments, you both may have to compromise at times.

Accepting Your Child's Temperament

There is more to temperament than just understanding it. Work on accepting your child's temperament. Acceptance helps you to avoid having unrealistic expectations of your child. Acceptance also can help prevent you from trying to make your child be someone she is not. Be willing to work with your child's temperament to help her develop in a healthy way.

Accepting your child's temperament may help you to get more rest, enjoy parenting more, and learn about yourself.

Sometimes it's difficult to accept your child's temperament. This especially is true if the temperament is different from your own. For example, you and your child may have different sleeping patterns. She may wake often, while you need lots of sleep. The key is to find a balance. Try to find some safe ways to keep your child entertained when she wakes up. For example, you might place a baby mirror on a nearby wall so she can look at herself. You may have to get out of bed to give your child some loving attention to get her back to sleep. Try to find something that works for all family members. It may take time and practice.

By understanding and accepting your child's temperament, you can help improve her behavior. Improvement does not mean perfection, however. Keep in mind that your child is learning how to act in life. Your understanding and acceptance are important to her success.

POINTS TO CONSIDER

What have you learned about your own temperament from reading this chapter? Explain.

If your child seems to have a low sensory threshold, should you expect her to enjoy new textures? Explain.

How can you help your child at a new day care if she is slow to adapt?

What does it mean to accept your child's temperament? How can your child benefit from your acceptance?

Chapter Overview

- Planning ahead for typical toddler behavior can help prevent a lot of problems. You can learn techniques to help your toddler behave in appropriate ways. These techniques all are based on respect for your child.

- It's important to understand your child's development. Focus on your child's positive behavior. Set limits for your child.

- It also is important to offer choices so your child feels a sense of control. Try to give your child attention before he misbehaves. Remove temptations from his path.

- Give your child advance warning of change. This helps him to cope with it.

- Let your child know what acceptable behaviors are.

CHAPTER 3

Preventing Behavior Problems

This chapter will help you prevent behavior problems in older infants and toddlers. For simplicity, we'll refer to this age group as toddlers. Curiosity drives most of a toddler's actions. Toddlers don't fully understand rules or warnings and usually do not behave badly on purpose. They do not try to annoy or embarrass you. In fact, toddlers often act without thinking. They have to be told things over and over before they begin to understand.

Preventing Problems
Planning ahead for typical toddler behavior can help prevent many problems. Following are techniques you can use to help your toddler behave in appropriate ways. These techniques all are based on respect for your child. They won't prevent all problems. However, they help you to help your child cope with the new and exciting things in his world.

Toddlers often want to do things for themselves. "Me do it" is a common phrase. Encourage your child when he wants to do things for himself. Give him a chance to put on his shoes or brush his own teeth. This way, he'll learn those skills sooner rather than later. Giving him the chance now will save you time in the future.

Understand Toddler Development

It's helpful for you to understand where your child is coming from. Toddlers need to explore their world. They like to run, climb, and touch. They get upset when you try to stop them. Toddlers imitate most things they see. They usually know what they want. They often try to tell or show you. They get frustrated if you don't understand.

Focus on the Positive

Often, your toddler may seem to be doing something that he shouldn't. Even if this is true, encourage and praise him when he is doing a good job. Make sure he knows what you are praising him for. Just saying "Good job" won't mean much to him. Be specific about the behaviors you are pleased with. Say, "Thank you for keeping your food on your tray" if he doesn't throw food as usual.

Giving frequent hugs and positive words helps your child learn what you expect from him. Remind your child often that you love him. Toddlers enjoy making their parents happy, so create an environment for your child that encourages appropriate behavior.

Here's a way to help prevent problem behavior in the kitchen. Give your child his own kitchen cupboard or drawer in a place that's easy to reach. Keep plastic bowls, wooden spoons, or his own toys in there. Rotate the supply often so he has new things to keep him busy.

Set Limits and Be Consistent

Begin with just a few reasonable expectations for your child to learn. Focus on two kinds of rules to begin with:

1. Those that keep your child safe

2. Those that stop him from hurting others and the environment

Your child needs to know that running into the street is unacceptable. Biting, kicking, or hitting others also are unacceptable behaviors. You always should respond to these behaviors. If you don't, your child may be confused about your expectations.

Some parents try to get their child to learn everything at once. But it is best to save bothersome behaviors for later. For example, don't worry if your child makes faces at others. Don't expect him to be polite at this age. Remember that he is just learning proper behavior. You can teach him more about acceptable behavior once he has learned the two kinds of rules mentioned previously.

Offer Choices

A great technique to use with toddlers and even older children is to offer choices. Instead of just saying, "You have to eat vegetables" say, "Would you like peas or carrots tonight?" Offering choices gives your child some power. It also limits his chance to say no to your requests.

Be careful not to offer too many choices. That much power can overwhelm toddlers. Opening a drawer and telling your toddler to choose a shirt could confuse him. Instead, lay out two shirts and ask him to choose one. Two choices are best at this age.

Give Your Child Attention Before He Misbehaves

Sometimes parents get so busy they forget to give their toddler enough attention. This especially may be true of teen parents who have a lot to juggle. Children who do not get enough attention may act out to get it. You can prevent this by making time to sit down and play. Choose activities you know your child enjoys. Even joining your child briefly can prevent an episode of misbehavior.

Toddlers like to explore. That's why their world should be a safe place. Here are some ways you can make your home safe for your child:

- Put safety locks on cupboards and drawers.

- Put breakable or unsafe items out of your child's reach.

- Use safety gates on stairs and unsafe rooms. (However, don't use accordion-style gates. These can trap and even strangle a child.)

- Use safety covers on electrical outlets.

MARGARET, AGE 16

"Sometimes when I'm busy with my homework, Regina starts acting up. It's like she knows that when I sit down at the computer, it takes away from her time with me. She pulls down my books, rips papers, and tries to grab pens and pencils. I've started to spend a good chunk of time with her before I do my homework. That seems to help. Sometimes I tape down some paper to the floor and give her big crayons to use while I study. I think she believes we are doing the same thing, so she doesn't try to get my attention."

Remove Temptations

Many parents of toddlers like to remove temptations from their child's path. You know about your toddler's curiosity. Therefore, it makes sense to put away things he shouldn't get into. Eventually, you can put things back in their original place. But while your child is a toddler, remove as many temptations as possible from his world. You won't have to say no as often. This can encourage him to explore freely.

Your toddler will act the way you act. If you yell, hit, or throw things, he will learn those behaviors. If you eat your vegetables, he's likely to eat his vegetables. Remember that you are a model for your child.

Give Advance Warning for Change

Toddlers rarely want to give up an activity they enjoy. The reality, however, is that they must. You can ease the change by warning your child beforehand. For example, don't just announce that it's time to leave the playground. Instead, tell your child 5 to 10 minutes in advance that you must leave soon. This gives him a chance to prepare mentally. He still may fuss, but over time, he will know what the warnings mean. Eventually, leaving will become more peaceful.

JACK, AGE 18

"Layla loves visiting my mom's house. My mom has two dogs and three cats. Layla plays with them constantly. She hates it when we have to leave. She screams and runs into Grandma's arms. I didn't used to tell her when it was time to leave. She'd scream on the bus for most of the way home. Now I tell her a few minutes before we have to leave. She still cries on our way out the door, but she gets control of herself faster. I'm glad. I'm sure people on the bus are glad, too!"

Focus on What Your Child Can Do

Often parents find themselves saying no to their toddler all day long. Move beyond that to tell your child what he can do. For example, avoid saying, "Don't squeeze the kitty." Instead, you can say, "You can touch the kitty this way." Then, show him with your own actions how to be gentle.

POINTS TO CONSIDER

What are the first two kinds of rules to set for your toddler? Why are these so important?

What are ways you can prevent toddlers from misbehaving?

What is important about offering your child choices at this age? Why shouldn't you offer too many choices?

If your child continues to tip over a plant in your mother's living room, what could you do?

- You can learn strategies for dealing with your child's misbehavior. Such strategies include redirection and a show of understanding. They also include use of natural and logical consequences and clear words and directions.

- Another technique some parents use is a time-out. Some experts do not believe time-outs should be used for children younger than 3.

- Spanking is *not* a technique for dealing with misbehavior. Children learn negative behavior if spanked.

CHAPTER 4

What to Do When Your Toddler Misbehaves

The prevention techniques you learned in the last chapter will go a long way. However, they won't prevent all problems. This chapter describes ways to deal with a toddler who is behaving unacceptably.

Redirect Misbehavior

If your child is doing something unacceptable, try to redirect her attention. Don't just scoop her up and move her away without offering anything new. Show respect by telling her that you understand she wants to touch the lamp. Then, tell her she can touch the flashlight instead.

You can even redirect your child if you see her heading for something unacceptable. Distract her before she reaches her destination. Prevention often is easier than acting afterward.

There are times when you need children to be quiet. Here are some ideas you can try:

■ Bring small toys or books for her to play with.

■ Bring a small snack that isn't too messy. Try crackers, cheese, or fruit.

■ Give your child as much attention as possible.

■ Point out objects in the room.

■ Play patty-cake or other quiet games.

■ Move to a place where you won't disturb others.

Show Your Child You Understand Her Feelings and Desires

Show understanding when your child is doing something unacceptable or is disappointed. For example, let's say you are outside playing but must go in to give your child a bath. Your child cries and yells because she doesn't want to go in. Show your child you understand her feelings. Say, "I know you want to stay outside. I can see that you're angry. But right now we need to take a bath."

Saying this will help your child realize it is okay to have feelings of disappointment or sadness. You can help her learn that even though she has these feelings, she still must let the activity go.

"I was watching another dad at the park yesterday. His kid fell down and hurt his elbow. The dad kept saying, 'Aw, quit crying. You're tough. What are you crying for? That didn't hurt.' I felt bad for the kid. His elbow probably did hurt, so why not cry for a while? When Joseph hurts himself, we say, 'Jeez, that must've hurt. It's okay to cry.' He doesn't seem to cry too long. It's almost as if he needs us to show we understand. Then he moves on to something new."

Use Natural and Logical Consequences, Not Punishment

If your child seems to misbehave on purpose, use natural and logical consequences. A consequence is the result of something a person does. For example, if your child is throwing food off the tray, say, "I see you've finished eating" and remove her from her eating space. Or, if she repeatedly hits the cat, say, "It is time to put the kitty outside. The kitty doesn't want to be hit." Notice that these are consequences, not punishments. After a while, your child will learn to connect the consequences to the behavior.

Use Clear Words and Actions

Shouting rarely helps you achieve your purpose with toddlers (or anyone). In fact, it can scare or confuse young children. Say, for example, that your child is throwing sand out of the sandbox. Instead of just shouting or saying, "No, no" say, "No throwing sand," and help her play peacefully in the sand. This way, she knows that you aren't saying no to the whole sandbox experience. You're just saying no to throwing sand.

Should You Redirect or Use a Time-Out?

Sometimes your child may misbehave in a way that could hurt herself or others. When this happens, let her know you don't approve. Look her in the eyes when you approach her. Tell her firmly that her actions weren't acceptable. Don't use too many words, or she'll lose the point of what you're trying to teach her. You may need to try to redirect her interests or use a time-out.

If your child is acting roughly, she may be imitating what she sees on TV. Limit the amount of TV your child watches, if any. If she is watching any TV at all, choose educational programs and watch with your child.

Some experts think time-outs shouldn't be used with children younger than 3. They think time-outs can do more harm than good, especially if children are left alone longer than 2 minutes. If you decide to use a time-out, remember only to use it for a serious offense, such as a child hurting another person or herself. A time-out isn't meant to be negative, and it isn't a form of punishment. Instead, it's a chance for a child to calm down or refocus. This is how a time-out works:

1. You've told your toddler not to touch the oven. However, she continues to do so.

2. Without raising your voice, say to her, "It is not okay to touch the oven. That's not safe for you." As you say this, pick her up with her back toward you.

3. Put her in her playpen or crib, but do so gently. Tell her she needs to relax for a couple minutes. Then leave her alone in the room.

4. Do not wait longer than two minutes to return to her. She may cry while you're gone, but the time-out helps her learn you are serious about the oven.

So what could you do instead of using a time-out? If you've used clear words and actions but she continues to touch the stove, redirect her interests. Give her plastic dishes she can "cook" with. Then prevent the behavior from happening the next time you cook. Give her safe items to "cook" with on the floor. That way she can feel like she is joining in your activity.

When your child seems to be misbehaving, ask yourself if he is misbehaving or simply trying to learn something new. Chances are, he is trying to learn. Use the moment to teach him what he needs to know.

Never Spank or Hit Your Child

Sometimes you may find yourself very frustrated with your toddler. It helps to take a few deep breaths and count to 10. You may need to ask someone you trust to care for your child for a while. It is never okay to hurt your child physically. It does more harm than good. If you hit, beat, pinch, slap, or kick your child, the following things can happen:

- Your child might learn that hurting others is okay.

- Your child could be seriously harmed because you may begin to use more physical force than you realize.

- Your child might see that she is getting your attention and may actually misbehave on purpose.

- Your child might be angry with you and want to get back at you.

"I told my family from the beginning that I wasn't going to spank Eli. Then one day when I came home from school, my mom said she had spanked him for coloring on the wall. My mom and I got in a huge fight. Eli and I ended up moving in with his dad's parents. They don't believe in spanking either. That's a better place for Eli and me."

POINTS TO CONSIDER

What are some techniques to use when your child misbehaves?

Describe a time-out. Why do you think some experts don't approve of using time-outs?

What would you do if your day care provider spanked your child for misbehaving?

Chapter Overview

- Sleeping is one of the issues parents often struggle with. Having a routine may make bedtime easier for your child. There are several ways to handle crying during the night.

- Temper tantrums are normal ways for toddlers to express anger. You can learn how to handle temper tantrums in private and in public.

- Toddlers often yell, scream, and whine. You can learn how to handle these behaviors.

- You can teach your child that exploring one's own body is healthy.

- Parents shouldn't punish children for toilet-training accidents.

CHAPTER 5

Areas of Special Concern
for Parents

Bedtime crying, temper tantrums, and yelling, screaming, and whining are some specific behaviors that often cause stress for parents. Some parents may not know how to react when children touch their own private parts. Toilet training is another area that sometimes causes parents stress. This chapter explains what you can do in these situations. It helps to remember that your child is just learning about appropriate behavior.

Problems at Bedtime and During the Night

Some infants have trouble falling asleep at night, and many toddlers dread going to sleep. You can expect your toddler to fuss a bit at bedtime. However, having a routine may make bedtime easier for both infants and toddlers. Try to do the same thing each evening. This may mean a bath and a story. You might try soft music. You may rock your child. These activities are soothing and will help your child to know that it's time to sleep.

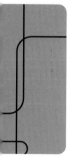

ELIOT, AGE 16

"Jared used to cry a lot before we put him in his crib at night. I decided to try reading to him for a few minutes right before bedtime. In just a few days, he cried a lot less. Now, he hardly ever cries before bedtime. When he sees me grab a book from his bookcase, I think he knows what it means: We're going to head for the rocking chair and read, and then he's going to bed."

Some parents don't feel comfortable leaving the room when their child cries at night. You also can try staying in the room. Stand by your baby's crib or lie next to it. Let him know you are there. You don't need to pick him up. Pat his back or talk with him in a soothing voice. This may help calm him.

Crying

Your child may cry when you put him to bed. The American Academy of Pediatrics (AAP) recommends letting your child cry 5 minutes before responding. Then, go in to comfort him for 1 minute without picking him up. Calmly and lovingly tell your child you love him and then leave. Wait another 5 minutes and repeat the steps as necessary. Crying that goes on for 20 minutes should be checked. It's possible your child may be sick or uncomfortable.

The AAP also recommends that you let your child cry a few minutes if he wakes during the night. He may go back to sleep. When you do go to his room, stay only a short time. You might rub his back or cuddle him. It is not, however, a good idea to bring him to your bed. Do not feed him unless you think he's hungry. If you do these things, he may expect them nightly and may not be able to sleep without them.

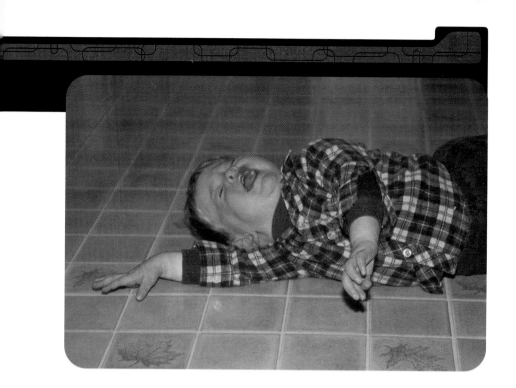

How to Handle a Temper Tantrum

Many parents have to deal with a child having a temper tantrum. During a tantrum, the child might throw himself on the floor and kick and scream. These are normal expressions of anger for a toddler. Remember that your toddler's fit is not directed at you. At this age, a child wants to make decisions and gets frustrated when he can't.

Your child may have a temper tantrum while you're at home. In this case, tell your child, "We need to be apart from each other right now to calm down." Then move to a different part of the room. If he follows you and continues his tantrum, call a time-out or redirect his interest. You can do this by putting him in a special chair you have saved for times like these. Then give him a couple books to look at. If you decide on a time-out, use it carefully. Remind your child and yourself that the time-out simply is a time to refocus and relax. It is not a form of punishment.

Tantrums are common at this age for the following reasons:

- Toddlers can't understand why they cannot touch, taste, and explore everything they want.

- Toddlers usually can't tell you in words what they want. This makes them angry.

- Toddlers react with strong emotions if they are tired, hungry, hot, uncomfortable, or wanting attention.

When your child's tantrum is over, don't dwell on it. Be firm but gentle if you need to repeat the request that started your child's tantrum. Being consistent shows your child that tantrums aren't effective.

When your child has a tantrum in public, it's tempting to give in to avoid being embarrassed. This is a bad idea. Giving in teaches your child that he can get what he wants by kicking and screaming. Don't let tantrums work for your child. If you do, it will mean more tantrums in the future.

If you are in public, it probably will help to hold your child in a tight hug until he calms down. You may need to take him out of the room. Public tantrums are hard to handle. Parents often feel embarrassed. Try to remember that your child is expressing emotions normally. Don't worry about what others think of your parenting. Your job is to be a good parent to your child in all situations.

Remember that it is your child's behavior that makes you angry, not your child. Here are ideas to help you calm down when you feel angry about a behavior:

- Count to 10 slowly. Think about something that makes you happy.

- Put your hands in your pockets. This will help keep you from using them on your child.

- Take a deep breath and let it out slowly.

- Move away from the situation. Go into another room or take a walk. Leave your child with someone you trust.

- Talk about the problem with your partner, parents, or a close friend.

Yelling, Screaming, and Whining

Toddlers often yell, scream, or whine. They may do this to try out their voice or to see how far they can push you. Try not to react strongly when your child does this. Teach him to use an "inside voice" when he yells or screams. Take him outside to yell or scream and tell him that is his "outside voice." He may think of it as a game. Then, inside, teach him to use a quiet voice by saying, "This is our inside voice."

If your toddler whines, remind him that he has a nice voice. Say, "Use your nice voice, please." It may take many times of repeating these requests. Your child eventually will learn not to yell, scream, or whine.

When Toddlers Touch Themselves

Around this age, your child will become aware of his body parts. When he discovers his genitals, he may touch them often. This wanting to touch the sex organs on the outside of the body is normal. By labeling, or naming, the genitals, you can help your toddler develop a healthy attitude about his body. For example, tell him, "That is your penis."

Your child may touch himself in public. If he does this, tell him he can do that at home in private. Then let him explore his body when at home. Try not to shame your child for touching himself. Exploring one's body is healthy.

Some children are ready to begin toilet training around their second birthday. They may show the following signs:

- Their diaper isn't always wet. This means their bladder is able to store urine, or liquid waste.

- They can follow directions.

- They can squat and stand up and have balance when walking.

- Their bowel movements have a fairly regular pattern.

- They use facial expressions, words, or gestures to show that their bladder is full. They use these expressions, words, or gestures when they're about to have a bowel movement, too.

- They show interest in imitating others in the bathroom.

- They are able to undress themselves.

Accidents During Toilet Training

Some children are ready to begin toilet training around age 2. However, many children do not begin toilet training until they are into their third year. Punishing your child for toilet training accidents is not a good idea. Children often cannot help it. And punishment does not help the child's self-esteem. Let your child know that you love him and you are trying to help him with this process. For more information on how to toilet train your child, see the book *Parenting a Toddler* in this series.

POINTS TO CONSIDER

What are some things you could try if your toddler cries when it is time for bed?

How can you teach your child not to yell? How can you teach him not to whine?

What would you do if you noticed your child touching his genitals while you were grocery shopping?

Why shouldn't you punish your child for accidents during toilet training?

- Sharing is not something most toddlers understand until around age 3 or 4. You can begin to teach your toddler about sharing and help her learn to play peacefully alongside other children.

- Many toddlers bite or hit out of anger. Sometimes they do these things just to see what happens. You can teach your child that both are unacceptable behaviors.

- Calling a child a "bad boy" or "bad girl" can hurt the child's self-esteem and can cause more behavior problems. Talk with your child in a way that won't hurt her self-esteem.

CHAPTER 6

Spending Time With Other Children

Sharing and playing with others are not skills children are born with. These skills must be taught. This chapter discusses sharing and how to talk with your child about sharing and kindness to others. It also covers what to do about aggressive behaviors such as biting and hitting.

Sharing

Sharing is not something most toddlers understand. Toddlers are egocentric. They think of themselves and not others. Because of this, they think of everything as "mine." This is not selfishness. It's normal human development. Your toddler won't begin to understand sharing until around age 3 or 4.

Problems arise when parents expect toddlers to share. Sometimes parents try to argue with their toddler about ownership. Unfortunately, this wastes your time. The following story illustrates this point.

Kevin and his daughter, Bernice, are playing by the toy box. Bernice picks up a bear and says, "Mine." Kevin replies, "No, that's not your teddy bear. That's Sidney's teddy bear." "MY teddy bear! Mine!" Bernice says. Her dad again says, "No, you've got Sidney's bear. Your teddy bear is upstairs. That is not yours." "MINE!" yells Bernice.

It isn't necessary to argue the way Kevin argues with Bernice. Instead, give your toddler accurate information. Kevin should say to his daughter, "I see you like Sidney's teddy bear. Would you like to play with it?"

Helping Your Child Learn About Sharing

Even though toddlers can't understand sharing, parents can begin teaching about it. Here's what you can do to help your child get ready for sharing:

- **Encourage and praise her when you notice her sharing.** This is true even if she holds something out to you but doesn't let go. She eventually will realize that sharing is positive. Say, "Thank you for sharing your snack with me."

When toddlers play, it usually is called "parallel play." They play near other children rather than with them.

- **Model sharing for her.** Show her that you are able to share things that are special to you. Label sharing when you do it or when you see it happening around you.

- **Have plenty of toys available when another child is around.** Doing this allows you to distract children who want a toy that someone else has. Ask the parents of other children to bring toys, too. That way, your child can play with something new instead of only offering all her toys.

- **Match playmates appropriately.** If possible, choose children who are similar in temperament to your child. Two aggressive children can probably handle the disputes. But pairing a quiet child with an aggressive one may not be fair.

- **Use a timer for older toddlers.** You can begin to show your toddler that sometimes it's necessary to give up a toy. Do this by setting a timer. When it goes off, announce, "Time to trade." Make sure each child gets handed something new. This won't go smoothly all the time, though.

- **Don't allow grabbing.** Most children simply grab toys from playmates. Discourage this behavior by showing your child how to ask for things. Explain how it makes others feel when your child grabs. For example, say, "Mari doesn't like it when you grab her toy." Teach your child how to extend her hands to show she wants something.

- **When necessary, separate children who are having problems sharing.** If two children cannot solve a sharing problem, separate them for a while. Chances are, they'll forget their troubles when reunited.

ANNA, AGE 17 AND SHERYL, AGE 16

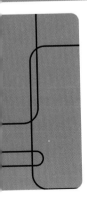

Anna and Sheryl often get their children together to play. Both kids are between 15 and 18 months. The two mothers realize their children don't know how to share just yet. So when there is a fight over a toy, one of the moms takes her child to another room. They stay away for about 5 minutes before returning. The toddlers always seem to forget that they had a dispute. The moms agree that at this age, this is the most peaceful way to solve sharing problems.

Here are some ways to prevent biting from happening:

- Watch for situations that you know upset your child.

- Change whatever your child is doing before she gets upset enough to bite.

- If your child is sleepy or hungry, try to keep her away from other children. These are times when biting is likely to occur.

Biting and Hitting

Many toddlers bite or hit. They may do this out of anger. They may do it to see what happens. Biting is developmentally appropriate for children ages 10 months to 2 years. However, you need to teach your child early that hurting others is unacceptable. Do this by telling her, "Use your words" or "People are not for hitting." Also tell her that biting hurts people: "Biting hurts daddy." Model gentle behavior early in your infant's life. This can help prevent biting and hitting during the toddler years. Show her how to stroke or gently touch others.

If your child does bite or hit someone, take immediate action. If you know your child won't bite you next, go to the victim first. It is important to comfort the child who has been bitten or hit. This takes attention away from the child who misbehaved and helps other children understand that such actions hurt others. Once your child has calmed down, talk with her about what happened. Tell her, "Biting hurts" or "Biting is not okay. Byron doesn't like it when you bite him."

Many parents give a time-out for incidents of biting to help the child settle down. If you choose to do this, tell your child she needs to relax in time-out for a few minutes before returning to play. Follow the steps outlined in Chapter 4.

Your child may not learn that biting and hitting are bad after only one incident. Be consistent in taking immediate action if she bites or hits someone again. Eventually, she will learn that these actions are not acceptable ways to behave.

Using the Right Kind of Language With Your Toddler

Calling a child a "bad boy" or "bad girl" can hurt his or her self-esteem. It actually can create more behavior problems. Even saying "Be nice" isn't a good idea because that implies that the child can "be bad." Instead of using those words, try saying "Be gentle."

Another way to talk with your child about behavior is to use language that reflects actions. For example, say, "I like how you are kind to Brenda" instead of saying, "You are so nice." Labeling someone "nice" isn't specific. At this point in your child's development, you should focus on specific actions.

Should you expect your 1-year-old to share with your cousin's 2-year-old? Why or why not?

What can you do to begin teaching your toddler to share?

What would you do if your day care provider repeatedly called your toddler a "bad girl" for not sharing?

At publication, all resources listed here were accurate and appropriate to the topics covered in this book. Addresses and phone numbers may change. When visiting Internet sites and links, use good judgment.

INTERNET SITES

ABC's of Parenting
www.abcparenting.com
Contains many articles on parenting divided by categories such as discipline, sleep, and toilet training

About.com—Parenting: Babies and Toddlers
http://babyparenting.about.com/parenting/babyparenting
Provides access to different articles and points of view on raising children

Baby Place
www.baby-place.com
Provides information on pregnancy, birth, and babies

KidsHealth
www.kidshealth.org
Has information on behavior and emotions, as well as health topics

Positive Approach to Discipline
www.ianr.unl.edu/pubs/Family
Provides information on positive discipline and how to do it

Your Amazing Baby
www.amazingbaby.com
Contains information on different development areas from birth to age 2

USEFUL ADDRESSES

American Academy of Pediatrics National
Headquarters
141 Northwest Point Boulevard
Elk Grove Village, IL 60007-1098
www.aap.org

Canadian Institute of Child Health
384 Bank Street
Suite 300
Ottawa, ON K2P 1Y4
CANADA
www.cich.ca

National Child Care Information Center
243 Church Street Northwest
2nd Floor
Vienna, VA 22180
1-800-616-2242
1-800-516-2242 (TTY)
www.nccic.org

The Nemours Foundation Center for Children's
Health Media
Alfred I. duPont Hospital for Children
1600 Rockland Road
Wilmington, DE 19803

Zero to Three: National Center for Infants,
Toddlers, and Families
734 15th Street Northwest
Suite 1000
Washington, DC 20005
www.zerotothree.org

FOR FURTHER READING

Endersbe, Julie. *Teen Fathers: Getting Involved*. Mankato, MN: Capstone, 2000.

Endersbe, Julie. *Teen Mothers: Raising a Baby*. Mankato, MN: Capstone, 2000.

Lindsay, Jeanne Warren. *Discipline From Birth to Three: How Teen Parents Can Prevent and Deal With Discipline Problems With Babies and Toddlers*. Buena Park, CA: Morning Glory Press, 1998.

Thoennes Keller, Kristin. *Parenting an Infant*. Mankato, MN: Capstone, 2001.

Thoennes Keller, Kristin. *Parenting a Toddler*. Mankato, MN: Capstone, 2001.

GLOSSARY

attachment (uh-TACH-muhnt)—the strong feeling of love that parents and children have for each other

bowel movement (BOUL MOOV-muhnt)—the act of ridding the body of solid waste

consequence (KON-suh-kwenss)—the result of an action

consistent (kuhn-SISS-tuhnt)—always the same, predictable

expectation (ek-spek-TAY-shuhn)—something considered reasonable or necessary of a person

genitals (JEN-i-tuhlz)—the sex organs located on the outside of the body

modeling (MOD-uhl-ing)—teaching by one's own actions or words

nurture (NUR-chur)—to tend to the needs of a child to help him or her grow and develop

redirection (ree-duh-REK-shuhn)—a discipline strategy; guiding a child toward a more acceptable behavior or activity than the one in which the child is currently involved

self-esteem (self-ess-TEEM)—a feeling of personal pride and respect for oneself

temper tantrum (TEM-pur TAN-truhm)—a fit of anger

temperament (TEM-pur-uh-muhnt)—the qualities and characteristics that contribute to one's personality

toilet training (TOI-lit TRANE-ing)—the process of teaching a child to use the toilet

toddler (TOD-lur)—a young child who has just learned to walk

INDEX